The Bear Who Stood on his Head

Ben could not know that as an adventurer he was a total disaster. While his brother and sister were sleek and nimble, he was as round as a butterball. While they viewed the world through shrewd coal-black eyes, Ben's were large and trusting, and the colour of chewed toffee.

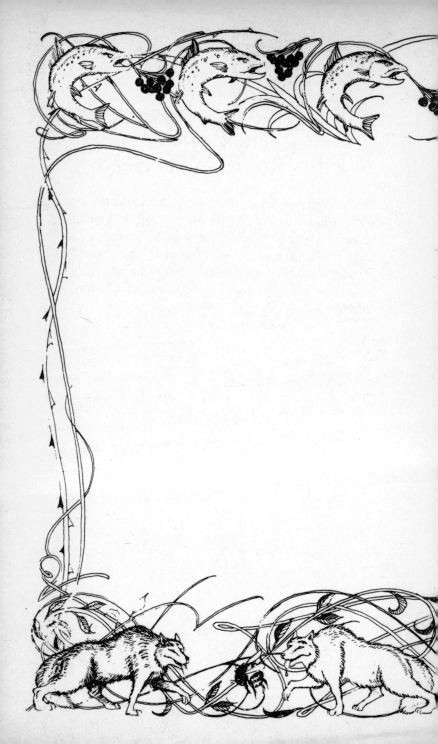

The Bear who Stood on his Head

W. J. CORBETT

Illustrated by Martin Ursell

mammoth

First published in Great Britain 1988
by Methuen Children's Books Ltd
Published 1989 by Mammoth
Reissued 1998 by Mammoth
an imprint of Egmont Children's Books Limited
Michelin House, 81 Fulham Road, London SW3 6RB

Text copyright © 1988 W. J. Corbett
Illustrations copyright © 1988 Martin Ursell

ISBN 0 7497 0032 7

10 9 8 7 6 5 4 3 2 1

A CIP catalogue record for this title
is available from the British Library

Printed in Great Britain
by Cox & Wyman Ltd, Reading, Berkshire

Contents

ONE

Ben's Spring Adventure

It was springtime in the Canadian wilderness. Everywhere the trees were in bud. It was time for two young grizzly bears to leave the family cave and explore a bright new morning world. First to emerge was Elspeth, dainty of step and shiny of coat. Close on her heels stalked Archibald, proud of eye and snooty of nose. Just as they were about to set off in search of adventure, they were halted in their tracks by their angry mother.

'What about Ben?' she cried, rushing to the mouth of the cave. 'Surely you're not going to leave him behind to get under my feet *again?* You know how he longs to go adventuring with you. I know he's fat and always tripping over his huge paws, but he is your brother. Don't you love him

any more?'

'Of course we love Ben,' wailed Elspeth. 'The truth is, me and Archibald love him more than we love ourselves. But Ben is always getting into dangerous scrapes, Mother, and we have to keep risking our lives to rescue him.'

8

'Of course we adore Ben,' added Archibald. 'It is just that me and Elspeth are sick and tired of shouting "Where are you, Ben?" – he seems to enjoy getting lost. Mother, you can't blame us for wanting to go adventuring without him.'

'I suppose you realise Ben is listening to every word?' shouted their mother angrily. 'I hope you can imagine how deeply your cruel words hurt him? You can guess what he's doing at this very moment . . .'

'We don't need reminding, Mother,' sighed Elspeth. 'As usual, Ben is standing on his head in a dark corner of the cave, weeping tears into his ears.'

'Ben is just a lovable blackmailer,' snapped Archibald. 'He's trying to melt our hearts so we'll take him with us.'

'Well, are your hearts melting?' shrilled their mother. 'Make up your minds quickly! The blood's rushing to his brain!'

'What can we say when we love him so?' said Elspeth helplessly. 'Very well, Mother, tell Ben to get down off his head and come up and join us.'

'But remind him that he must do exactly what we say this time,' warned Archibald. 'He must promise to leave all the risky stunts to me and Elspeth.'

From below, they heard a triumphant shout and then a dull thud as Ben toppled to the ground. Moments later he came blundering out of the cave, brushing aside his beaming mother and sending his brother and sister flying as he hugged them in gratitude. Lovingly, he helped them to their feet, his eyes shining as he waited for the adventure to begin . . .

Ben could not know that as an adventurer he was a total disaster. While his brother and sister were sleek and nimble, he was as round as a butterball. While they viewed the world through shrewd, coal-black eyes, Ben's were large and trusting, and the colour of chewed toffee. But it was from those unusual eyes that Ben's true character shone. His eyes were the windows of a soul prepared to love everything and everyone. And because

Ben was so filled with love, he was doubly loved in return.

But back to the adventure. Elspeth and Archibald loved Ben, but they still grumbled when they had to wait for him to catch them up.

'If only Ben wasn't so overweight,' complained Archibald, as they squatted on the pine-needled path and waited for him.

'I know, but his heavy and earnest panting is music in our ears,' said Elspeth,

her black eyes
shining with love,
as Ben finally slumped
exhausted beside them.
He looked so pleased that they both had
to give him a bear-hug. At long last, after
many more stops to wait for Ben, they
arrived at the salmon stream.

'Now listen carefully, Ben,' said Archibald, sternly. 'Our spring adventure can
begin. Me and Elspeth are going to ven-

ture out into mid-stream. We plan to get there by leaping from jutting rock to jutting rock to avoid the treacherous rapids. Once we're both perched on a boulder, we will plunge our paws into the water and try to snag some salmon. Ben, this is your vital role. You must stay safely on the shore and act as look-out. What you look out for is not important. What *is* is that you keep your paws dry. In other words, Ben, just leave the salmon-fishing to us. If you promise to do as we say, we'll bring you a tasty fish.'

Elspeth looked anxiously at her young brother and said firmly, 'If you disobey us, we'll send you straight home to Mother. Is that clear, Ben?'

But the plump little bear was only half-listening. His toffee-coloured eyes were gazing out over the water, drinking in the majestic sight of the waves dashing and foaming about the rocks in mid-stream. There was sadness in his soft eyes, too. For he was noticing the silver fishes twisting desperately through the air, as they tried to leap the falls to reach their spawning grounds in the calmer reaches upstream. Many of them failed and fell back exhausted. This upset Ben so much that his brother and sister's orders were the last straw. Ben stood on his head and tears sprang into his eyes and trickled into his ears.

Archibald had no choice.

'We aren't saying you can't paddle in the shallows, Ben,' he soothed. 'But you must swear not to wade out above your ankles.'

'If you do, you'll be tempted to get your knees wet, then your nose, and you'll end up drowned,' explained Elspeth, worried out of her mind. 'So, Ben, will you pro-

mise to keep your knees bone-dry?'

At once, their brother was right-way up, with tear-soaked eyes smiling the sunniest smile in the world and Elspeth and Archibald rushed to hug him again.

Then Elspeth and Archibald leapt in turn on to the first stepping-stone that jutted above the swirling water. Soon they were sprawled on adjoining rocks, happily snatching the fish and gorging themselves on the rich red flesh. They

quite forgot about Ben until Elspeth just happened to glance towards the shore. Suddenly she sat bolt upright, her eyes filled with concern.

'Archibald, I can't see Ben paddling in the shallows,' she cried. 'And the shore is completely deserted. What's happened to our lovely brother, and our mother's favourite son?'

Panic-stricken, Archibald gazed at shore and shallows. But his shrewd black

eyes saw nothing to boost his sinking heart.

'Ben must have disobeyed our orders,' he yelled above the racket of the surging waves. 'He must have waded out above his ankles and his knees, right up to his nose and been swept away by the fierce currents. Quickly, Elspeth, we must leap from rock to rock back to the shore and race downstream and save Ben before he's dashed to pieces on the sharp rocks below . . .'

Scrambling ashore, they were soon bounding along the bank at top speed trying to out-race the sea-bound currents, shouting, 'Ben, Ben!' After covering two breathless miles, they saw him. They need not have worried. Ben was very much alive. Suddenly they felt very angry. Ben was bobbing up and down in a sucking whirlpool, without the slightest sign of fear, as it tried to drag him down to a watery grave. Gasping for air, his smile never once faltered as his clumsy but tender paws helped the more tired salmon to leap the towering rapids. As for the fish who were too weak to attempt that gigantic leap, many felt the comforting stroke of his loving paws as they wallowed on their sides, waiting for death. But the plight of the salmon was the last thing on the minds of Elspeth and Archibald as they gazed out over that crashing dash of water.

'Ben,' shouted a relieved but angry Archibald. 'This is an order. Stop wasting your love on salmon and think about our love for you. Not to mention Mother, whose favourite you are!'

'If you don't stop doing good deeds for fishes, we'll be forced to risk our lives and dive in to rescue you,' cried Elspeth, wringing her paws on the dry bank. 'So make your choice, Ben. Are you prepared to sacrifice me and Archibald for the sake of the odd, unlucky salmon who can't leap as high as his friends?'

Tearfully, for not even the fury of the waves could wash away his tears, Ben paddled to the shore to safety. He knew he was in disgrace, so he did what he

always did when he was upset. He stood on his head and wept tears into his ears.

'Ben, for your own good we are sending you straight home to Mother,' said Archibald, steeling his heart. 'And also for the good of me and Elspeth. Your conduct this morning has made us two bags of nerves.'

'And when you get home, remember to tell Mother that you brought this banishment on yourself,' chimed in Elspeth, equally firmly. 'So what are you waiting

for? On your way, Ben, we've had enough of you for one day.'

With a sodden thud, their tubby brother hit the ground and stood upright. Still weeping, he shambled off home, his stumpy tail tucked miserably between his legs. Once he paused on the skyline to stand on his head, only to continue his sad journey till he was lost from view. Elspeth and Archibald were moved to tears.

'You may well hang your heads,' scolded Mother when they eventually returned home, tired out. 'I hope you can explain why Ben arrived home hours ago, all soaking wet and weeping?'

'Ben is lucky to be alive after all the trouble he caused,' said Archibald, his temper flaring.

'And so are we, Mother,' said Elspeth, her feelings also ruffled. 'For we were nearly forced to put our lives on the line in order to save Ben from his own foolishness.'

But Mother wasn't interested in their

excuses and sent them to bed. Still smarting from her harsh words, Elspeth and Archibald curled up in the cave and tried to sleep. But a quiet sobbing made them toss and turn for most of the night. Ben was standing on his head in his favourite corner, grieving that he had lost their love, and weeping tears into his ears . . .

TWO

Ben's Summer Adventure

Summer came to the Canadian wilderness. Everywhere, the trees were in leaf. For two young grizzly bears it was time to leave the family cave to explore a hot new morning world. Daintily, Elspeth emerged, closely followed by Archibald, his snooty nose sniffing the sweet air. Just as they were about to set off on their travels, they were hailed by their vexed mother.

'So, Ben is saddled with being a stay-at-home again, is he?' she cried, her large bulk framed in the entrance to the cave. 'I suppose you two were trying to sneak off and leave me to cope with his snivelling? I don't need to tell you what he's doing, do I?'

'And you want us to tell Ben to get down off his head and come up and join us,' said Archibald, fed up. 'Are me and Elspeth to be blackmailed for ever, Mother?'

'If only we didn't love Ben so much,' sighed Elspeth. 'If only we could bring ourselves to hate him. Then we could march off without a backward glance. But we can't, so we won't. Very well, we give in. Tell Ben that me and Archibald are waiting up top for him and his nuisance.'

'But this time he must cross his heart and swear to obey our instructions,' insisted Archibald. 'Tell him that this time we are in deadly earnest.'

Hurriedly, Mother, Elspeth and Archibald leapt aside as Ben came rushing pell-mell from the cave, anxious to hug his brother and sister who loved him again. Embracing empty air, he promptly fell on his large pink nose. Not at all put out, he picked himself up and gazed adoringly at the nervous pair.

Soon he was waddling along behind them, eager to find out what adventure lay in store for him. Half an hour later, the trio were entering a small copse. When they arrived at a clearing in the centre, Archibald ordered Ben to squat on his haunches in the shade of a lone tree.

'Now, Ben, we are sitting beside the trunk of the honey tree,' he began solemnly. 'I will now explain our adventure to you. I am going to climb to the top and swarm out along that fragile branch. If you glance up, you'll notice that at the end of it a honey-bee nest is hanging. Elspeth will perch on that stout branch just a little lower down than mine, shout insults and pull ugly faces to distract the angry bees, while I slip a paw inside their nest and steal a dollop of honey. Now, Ben, this is your important job. While we are up the tree, you will be sitting here on the ground, waiting for the honey-dollop to plop into your outstretched paw. Now, doesn't your vital role make you tingle with excitement?'

But the happy light in Ben's toffee-coloured eyes had faded. Ben knew he was being fobbed off with a safe but dull job. There was only one thing to do. He stood on his head and began to sniffle and snuffle.

'Very well, Ben,' said Archibald, controlling his temper. 'You can climb the honey tree. But only as high as the lowest branch. Once you're firmly seated, you must promise to cling on tightly with

three paws. Use your free one to catch the dollop of honey as it comes hurtling down. Have you got that, Ben?'

For answer, Ben performed an awkward forward roll to stand dizzily on his rear paws. And his smile was as sweet as the honey they meant to pinch. A minute later, Ben began to climb after his nimble brother and sister, puffing and panting.

'I am nearly at the end of the fragile branch, Elspeth,' called Archibald. His voice trembled a little, for the limb he clung to was beginning to creak and groan. 'Start shouting insults and pulling faces at the bees as quickly as possible, I've been stung three times already.'

'How can I, when I'm sobbing at a sight that's breaking my heart, and will probably break your neck?' wept Elspeth from lower down. 'As usual, Ben has disobeyed us. He's crawling out along your fragile branch. If you weren't in such a dangerous position, I'd ask you to crane back over your shoulder and see for yourself. Please God, protect you both! Ben is just behind you, smiling and nudging at your tail.'

'Order him to go back,' yelled a frightened Archibald. 'Warn him that this branch will break. Be firm, Elspeth. Wag

30

an angry paw and shout that if he doesn't do as he's told, we'll send him straight home to Mother.'

'It's too late to hammer sense into Ben's head,' moaned Elspeth, sensing disaster. 'Anyway, he's enjoying himself too much to obey me. While some of the bees are stinging you and me, others are buzzing around Ben's nose, feeding him honey. They love him as much as everyone does, even though they must know he's a honey bandit in league with us. Archibald! The

31

twig you and Ben are clinging to is about
to snap! Jump and parachute-roll as you
hit the ground. You've got to gasp at Ben
to do the same. I can't warn him, there's a

cloud of bees renewing their attack on me
. . . ouch . . . ouch . . .'

Archibald was still shouting warnings to Ben as he and his brother plunged earthwards. Thanks to a skilful landing, Archibald escaped with a few cuts and bruises. As for Ben, no parachute-roll for him. He left his fate, as he did everything, in the lap of the gods. And, not surprisingly, even the gods loved Ben. For, cushioned by their grace, and by his own rolls of fat, he merely bounced harmlessly on the hard floor of the wood.

'It's straight home to Mother for you, Ben,' snapped Archibald, rubbing his cuts and bruises and bee-stings.

'And don't forget to tell her that you brought this disgrace on yourself,' added Elspeth, swarming down the tree and scratching at her own painful stings. 'And if Mother rants and raves about our sending you home early, please confess how you almost got yourself and Archibald killed. Now be off with you.'

Hardening their hearts and scratching

their wounds, they watched their fat little brother lumber away, sniffing and wiping the tears from his nose.

Some time later, they also arrived home to face the music.

'So,' said their mother, grimly. 'Once again you've cut short your brother Ben's adventurous day out. How dare you send him home with his smart whiskers dripping sweet honey and tears?'

'Mother, don't you care even a jot for me and Elspeth?' cried Archibald. 'Don't you realise that we also love Ben, even though he ruins all our adventures. Ben's tears are all very well, but just look at our bee-stings and bruises.'

'Which itch terribly,' said Elspeth, looking ready to cry.

'Of course I care for both of you,' Mother answered sharply. 'But you know full well that your younger brother can't cope with the harshness of life as you two can. That's why I rely on you to look after him. But off to bed, I'm really angry with you. Poor Ben won't get much

36

sleep tonight. I suppose you know where
he is . . . ?'

Archibald and Elspeth knew exactly

where Ben was. They also knew exactly what he was doing. Before they fell into an exhausted sleep, they could see quite clearly on the cave wall the shadow of Ben standing on his head, weeping copious tears into his ears . . .

THREE

Ben's Autumn Adventure

Autumn came to the Canadian wilderness. Everywhere, the trees were shedding leaves. For two young grizzly bears, it was time to leave their family cave to explore a mellow morning world. Just as Elspeth and Archibald were about to set off along The Trail of The Lonesome Pine that snaked up into the high hills, the indignant voice of their mother came shrilling up from the depths.

'How long must Ben suffer for his past mistakes?' she cried. 'I know he can be vexing, but don't you cruel pair of bears care that he hasn't been taken out on an outing since last summer? Must he stay cooped up below ground for ever? Why won't you take him for a brisk walk to get some fresh air into his stuffy lungs?'

'You know why, Mother,' shouted Elspeth. 'If we took Ben with us, he'd spoil our adventure. It's about time Ben realised what a lucky bear he is to have a brother and sister who are prepared to put up with his unlucky presence.'

'Does that mean Ben is in luck? You're prepared to take him from beneath my busy paws? Quite frankly, having Ben standing on his head at home can be a trial when I've so much to do.'

40

The two young gizzly bears realised that they had fallen neatly into Mother's trap.

'Very well, Mother,' Archibald said, wearily. 'We will take Ben with us. But you must stress to him that this is his last chance. Warn him that if he strays from the path of obedience once more, he'll be sent straight home to stand on his head for ever.'

'We mean it, Mother,' chimed in Elspeth, sternly. 'You must first make him realise we're not made of patience and that only our love makes us ignore the warnings in our heads.'

The words were hardly out of her mouth before Ben came shambling from the cave, sending his brother and sister flying like ninepins as he gave them an affectionate pat each. Moments later, he was waddling along behind them as they set out along The Trail of The Lonesome Pine. Elspeth and Archibald were still staggering and counting stars. But Ben's toffee-coloured eyes were wide and clear

as he drank in the beauty of the looming heather-clad slopes, and enjoyed the springy feel of soft mosses beneath his large flat paws. An hour or so later, the three bears arrived at the high hills and gratefully slumped down for a breather. When they had recovered, Archibald turned to Ben.

'We are now sitting on top of mouth-watering Blueberry Hill, Ben,' he said,

wiping the dribble from his chops. 'And why are our mouths watering? Because all around us are blueberry bushes loaded down with plump sweet fruit. But a word of caution, Ben. Bushes that sag with deliciousness hate plundering grizzly bears. That is why every one is intertwined with thorny blackberry brambles to keep the likes of us away. But though me and Elspeth have ways and means of getting at the tempting blueberries, you haven't. So, Ben, as you've promised with all your heart to obey us this time, will you stay exactly where you are and leave the blueberry picking to us?'

'Please give us your solemn word, Ben,' pleaded Elspeth. 'For Mother will only bawl us out if we're forced to order you home alone, all ripped to pieces on the vicious thorns.'

Ben's lovely eyes were suddenly mournful. He had been hoping to be allowed to tackle the thorny bushes in a daredevil fashion.

'Don't forget Ben's second crucial role in the adventure, Elspeth,' hastened Archibald, noting the brooding look in his brother's eyes. 'His really important role is to sit and point out with his paw the sweetest and plumpest berries for us to pick. Then, with our arms full of them, we will rush back to share them with our chief scout, whose name is Ben.'

But Ben wasn't fooled for a moment. At once his face crumpled and tears welled

into his toffee-coloured eyes. Before he could stand on his head, his brother and sister were at his side, anxious to comfort him.

'Ben could sniff at the berries,' said Elspeth, wiping away Ben's tears with a tender paw. Then, looking sternly at her young brother, 'But only to sniff at them, mind.'

Instantly, Ben was smiling his heart-melting smile through his tears. Happy again, he rose and lumbered off to sniff at the things he was allowed to sniff at. Trustingly, Elspeth and Archibald left him to it and trotted away to brave the sharp thorns that protected the blueberries from grizzly bear thieves. Just then, a storm broke over Blueberry Hill. As the rain pelted down and the lightning flashed and the thunder rolled, Elspeth suddenly remembered Ben. She glanced around, her heart sinking as she failed to glimpse him. Sheltering beneath a blueberry bush, she shouted across to Archibald, who was cowering beneath a bush nearby. Through cupped and blue-stained paws, she hurled an urgent message.

'Can you see Ben, Archibald?' she cried above the roar of thunder. 'The last time I saw him, he was sniffing at the berries on that large bush over there. Pray to God he hasn't been struck by a bolt of lightning, and is now lying on his back, paws in the air, his fur burnt to a crisp.'

From the shelter of his own bush, Archibald wiped the streaming rain from

his eyes and peered wildly around. And then he saw.

'Ben is quite safe, Elspeth,' he yelled. 'At least, his rear portion is. Through the driving rain I can just make out his fat behind poking out of that large bush. Though I dread to think where his front portion has got to!'

'I can see him, too,' called back Elspeth. 'I think Ben's front portion is inside the bush, which can only mean that he's disobeyed our orders again. In other words, Ben is half-way out and also half-way in the bush.'

'Well, no half measures for us, Elspeth,' shouted Archibald. 'We must risk the fury of the storm and save our disobedient darling brother from starving to death. And you know who'll get a roasting from Mother if her favourite son should dwindle to a dry skeleton?'

Imagining Mother's angry face, the two worried bears emerged from their shelters and dashed across to Ben's bush. Poking her head into its dark depths, Elspeth was puzzled by the sight that met her eyes.

'Archibald, come look,' she urged in a muffled voice. 'Ben's head is caught in a crown of thorns, yet he's smiling his beautiful smile. Surely, not even our adorable brother can be that saintly.'

Mystified, Archibald eased his head inside the bush to join hers. Then, suddenly angry, he said, 'And we were afraid that Ben would die from hunger, Elspeth. Can't you see those two robins hopping from twig to twig around his head? That is why Ben is smiling. Those birds are busily pushing blueberries into his

mouth. How can it be that the most trying grizzly bear in the whole of Canada is so very much loved, even by strangers? But then, as simple bears, me and you can only ask hard questions, Elspeth. We must leave the answers to wiser minds. Our task is to extract Ben from the bush. So, soaked to the skin and afraid of the lightning, are we prepared to do our duty, Elspeth?'

'Of course,' cried Elspeth, shivering in

the cold driving rain. 'I can just see Mother's furious face if we fail. But listen, I've the perfect plan. If you grab hold of Ben's tail and I grab hold of yours, all we need to do is to dig in our heels and pull with all our might!'

It worked. Moments later, the three bears were strung out in a paw-to-tail chain, Elspeth and Archibald heaving with all their might. After much puffing and panting, Ben's front portion was

finally drawn from the bush like a cork from a bottle. But a very raggedy cork, alas. Yet he seemed not to care, as he chomped away at a mouthful of juicy berries kindly provided by the robins, for his smile was as wide as ever. Then, before Elspeth and Archibald had time to loosen their grip on the tail in front, a mischievous lightning bolt hurtled down from the sky. The tingling charge entered Elspeth's tail and ran through her body,

then entered Archibald's tail and ran through his body, but strangely fizzled out when it reached Ben's tail.

Yelling with shock, the fur on their backs standing on end like the quills on a porcupine, Archibald and Elspeth realised with awe what they had long suspected: nothing in Heaven or on Earth could harm their brother Ben. But charmed life or no, the two bears were as angry with him as they had ever been.

'Ben, get out of our sight before we forget how much we love you,' fumed his brother, wincing in pain as he brushed sparks from his singed pelt. 'We might have known that you'd do your own thing and nearly get us killed again.'

'And tell Mother that me and Archibald are not responsible for your appearance,' wept Elspeth, glancing at her own once silky fur, now sizzled and wild-looking, adding, 'And if Mother complains that you look as if you've been dragged through a bush backwards, tell her it's because you have! Tell her that we were forced to take drastic action. Tell her that we will be returning home later as singed heroes. And now, go home, it's dangerous to be near you.'

'But don't worry, we'll love you as much as ever when our tempers cool,' said Archibald, sighing with relief as he plumped his red-hot bottom into a pool of rain-water. Then, glancing up, 'So what are you waiting for, Ben?'

Ben was still hoping that he could continue the day's adventuring. But when he saw their stern looks, tears welled up into his astonishingly beautiful toffee-coloured eyes. He knew he was truly in their bad books, so he waddled off home, scratched and minus a large tuft of fur and most of his whiskers. Twice he stopped to stand on his head to weep tears into his ears before he vanished from view.

As for Elspeth and Archibald, they didn't feel like any more adventuring that day. Instead, they spent the afternoon slumped on Blueberry Hill recovering from shock, and worrying about what

Mother would say when she saw them. As evening began to fall, they plucked up their courage and limped back to the cave. The greeting they received confirmed their worst fears.

'What's the meaning of sending Ben home soaked to the skin and half-scalped?' shrilled Mother. 'Even if he escapes flu, his good looks are ruined for life. What has your adventuring done to my Ben?'

'You mean what has Ben's adventuring

done to us,' protested Elspeth. 'Didn't Ben tell you that we were struck by lightning while we were trying to rescue him from the blueberry bush?'

'Which is why his fur is singed and still standing on end,' explained Archibald. 'Mother, don't you care about your two older bear cubs at all?'

'Of course I care for each one of my three bears,' replied Mother sharply. 'But will caring for you two grow back Ben's whiskers and heal his wounds in record time? I doubt it. Now if his older brother and sister had taken care of him properly, he wouldn't have come home in such a state. But I'm not wasting any more words. You can both go to bed at once! I'm disappointed in you. Don't forget to give Ben a loving pat before you drop off. He thinks you hate him for some reason.'

Tired and still tingling from the effects of the lightning bolt, Elspeth and Archibald limped down into the gloomy cave. After wishing Ben a genuine and tender 'Good night', and giving his upturned soles a loving pat, they curled up and fell fast asleep. Soon, the cave was filled with the sound of whistling snores and the quiet sobs of a small plump bear who stood on his head in his favourite corner, weeping tears into his ears . . .

FOUR

Ben's Winter Adventure

Winter came to the Canadian wilderness. Everywhere, the trees stood stark and leafless against the sky. For two young grizzly bears it was time to leave the family cave to go exploring a crisp and snowy morning. Teeth chattering, paws stamping, Elspeth and Archibald were just about to set off for the Ghostly Wood when they were stopped in their tracks by the voice of their furious mother.

'You're not the only bears who love snow, you know,' she cried. 'Your brother Ben is itching to feel its crispness beneath his flat paws. Do you hate him so much? Shame on you both. There he is standing on his head in his corner, babbling promises to obey your every command, and what do you two do? You turn

your backs on him. Why?'

'Because Ben never learns his lesson, that's why,' retorted Elspeth, hardening her soft heart. 'How many times has he promised to be good, only to turn out bad?'

'We're not going to stand for Ben's blackmailing this time,' vowed Archibald. 'Can you give us one good reason why we should trust Ben's promises, Mother, after all the dangers we have endured for his sake?'

'I can give you the most perfect reason in the world,' answered their mother,

sharply. 'I will vouch with my life that he is a thoroughly changed bear. In fact he's now so good as gold that you won't even know he's with you. So are you, or are you not going to give Ben one last chance?'

'If Ben is honestly prepared to do as we say . . .' said Archibald reluctantly. Then, 'Oh very well, Mother. We'll take

your word that Ben has given his word to behave this time.'

'Does that mean "Yes"?' said their eager mother. 'Only I'm dying for a bit of peace and quiet.'

'Yes, go and shout the glad tidings in

Ben's wet ears,' replied Elspeth, biting her lip and wondering whether they were not making a terrible mistake. But there was no time to think before Ben came bowling out of the cave to join them, his plump face wreathed in smiles.

He was so happy that he playfully

cuffed at the snow-drift they were standing on. It was Ben's first dangerous mistake of the day. Suddenly, a mini-avalanche rolled down the hill, completely burying his brother and sister. Tenderly, Ben dug them out before they suffocated. Shaking and shivering with shock, Elspeth and Archibald gazed fearfully at Ben, dreading what danger he might put them in next. But Ben just gazed at them, his trusting toffee-coloured eyes glowing with excitement, as he waited for the adventure to begin. When their legs had stopped shaking like jelly, Elspeth and Archibald set off through the deep snow and Ben followed faithfully in their paw prints.

Soon they were entering the Ghostly Wood.

'Now, Ben,' said Archibald, slowly and carefully. 'We three bears are huddled together for comfort in the middle of Ghostly Wood. Can you feel the fur prickling on the back of your neck? That's because we're frightened. So, Ben, as this

is to be our bravest adventure of all, you must obey every instruction. Me and Elspeth are going to dash about shouting insults and cheeky challenges at the evil spirits who lurk amongst the trees. Then, when they spring out at us, screaming and vowing to tear us limb from limb, we will flee for our lives. While me and Elspeth are racing about in terror, you must sit here as still as a stone, not daring even to breathe an unkind word at the evil spirits. If they saw you, they'd easily catch you because you're so plump and slow, Ben.

So remember, just stay here looking like an innocent brown boulder, clenching your paws as you silently encourage me and Elspeth to outwit and outrun the evil spirits. Isn't it an exciting plan, Ben? You'll do what we say, won't you?'

'The plan won't work unless you sit here with your mouth shut tight,' said Elspeth, who was praying that Ben wouldn't make difficulties. 'Don't forget, you've promised to be an obedient brother this time. So can we count on you to remain a harmless onlooker?'

The excited look faded from Ben's face. Twin tears glistened in his toffee-coloured eyes as he forward-rolled into a headstand.

'Perhaps if we allowed Ben to amble amongst the trees in a good-natured way?' said Archibald, desperately. 'And maybe stick out his tongue in an impish and friendly fashion? Surely the evil spirits wouldn't take offence at that?'

'So long as Ben sticks out his cheeky tongue half-way only,' replied Elspeth,

not at all keen on the idea. 'And he doesn't let his good-natured amble become a challenging strut, and sticks to the sunlit parts of the wood, and avoids the dark creepy spots like mad, the evil spirits shouldn't mind. But will Ben agree to this new plan?'

For answer, Ben's face lit up again as he backward-rolled to regain his large flat paws. Smilingly, he nodded his agreement.

Reassured, the older bears romped away to taunt evil spirits. Ben rolled along behind them and poked out his tongue all the way. Disobedience came naturally to him. Then suddenly, pretend fear became real fear for the three bears. A pack of snarling, hungry wolves came through the trees. Scenting the bear-cubs , they tracked them down and surrounded them. Though trembling with fear, Elspeth and Archibald reacted without thinking. Stoically, they prepared to sacrifice their own lives in order to save their beloved brother and their mother's favourite. Heartlessly, because he was full of heart, Archibald turned on his smiling brother.

'Ben, crash through the ring of wolves and go straight home, and do not look back,' he snapped, harshly. Then he added what he believed would be his last lie on earth. 'Me and Elspeth are sick and tired of your company and wish to play with the wolves without you spoiling the fun.'

'Though we do wish you God speed, Ben,' cried Elspeth hysterically. 'And if you do manage to blunder through the ring of wolves and reach home, remember to tell Mother that you haven't a hair out of place because we refused to let you play rough games with the wolves. And if me and Archibald are late home from this adventure, tell her that it's because we loved you more than we loved ourselves. She'll understand, weepily we hope. So what are you waiting for, Ben? Don't give us that sad, far-away look. Run away, we want to begin our private game with the wolves.'

The leader of the wolf-pack seemed to agree. His teeth were no longer bared. Now he was smiling and wagging his tail like a puppy-dog as he waited for Ben to dash from the circle to safety. He even trotted aside to give the tubby bear room, and raised his paw to give Ben a loving pat as he sped by, for even fierce Canadian wolves can fall in love. And hungry though they were, the whole pack was in

no doubt that the bear with the toffee-
coloured eyes was definitely Top of their
Pops. But Ben refused to budge. He was
fed up with always being sent home just
when the adventure became exciting.

When he saw Ben slump stubbornly on
his backside, the chief wolf lost patience.

Snarling again, he signalled for the pack
to close in. Instantly, Elspeth and Archibald were knocked to the ground and
were fighting for their lives. On the orders
of the chief wolf, Ben was left strictly
alone. He still thought the whole thing
was a game and that, as usual, he'd been

left out of it, so there was only one thing
left to do. Ben stood on his head and the
tears trickled into his ears.

The wolves were so shocked they
stopped savaging Elspeth and Archibald.
The sight of Ben in tears filled them with
remorse. Their hunger pangs no longer
mattered. They realised that if they ate
Elspeth and Archibald, they would
always be denied Ben's love. The wolves
drew back from Elspeth and Archibald
and gazed expectantly at Ben. He forward

rolled and, still weeping, set off for home. He could be obedient after all. He had finally decided to do what his brother and sister told him. But though Ben was used to arriving home alone, it still upset him dreadfully. He was weeping as he shambled past the sobbing Elspeth and Archibald, and the huddle of moist-eyed wolves. But this journey home was not like the others. For the first time in his short life, Ben came home in triumph.

Flanked on the right by a proud Archibald, and on the left by an adoring Elspeth, Ben was as happy as he could be. Flying in attendance above him, the faithful robins busily stuffed sweet red berries into Ben's smiling mouth to keep him topped up with nourishment. And to complete the party came the wolves. They spread out fan-wise behind to prevent any sneaky attack by another pack who had nothing to love in the world. Though Ben enjoyed all the fuss, he had no idea what he had done to deserve it. But he loved it all the same. His huge

73

toffee-coloured eyes glowed with plea-sure as the party neared the family cave, for he longed to see mother's face when she saw him coming home for the first time not alone.

Mother was waiting at the mouth of the cave. She was astonished. Nervous, too for she didn't think much of wolves. After Elspeth and Archibald had gasped out the amazing events of the morning, she looked vastly relieved . . . and smug. After the wolves had howled a warm 'goodbye' before sloping off to track down a moose for tea; after the robins had flown away to their evergreen bush, to escape the terrible winter chill by tuck-ing their heads under their wings, poor things, Mother, in the depths of the cave, voiced her happy thoughts.

'Who would have thought that Ben would make good some day?' she said dreamily. 'Who would have believed that my little fat cub would turn out to be a hero amongst grizzly bears?'

'I think the word "hero" is a but much,

Mother,' protested Archibald. 'I think "lucky" is the word for Ben.'

'"Lovably lucky" is our Ben in a nut-shell,' agreed Elspeth. 'For though he saved us from the wolves, he didn't really mean to. It just happened that way.'

'Are you suggesting that next spring Ben won't be in charge of all future adventures?' bristled Mother. 'Are you hinting that he'll be a stay-at-home nuisance when we wake from our long winter

76

sleep, and stay under my paws when I'm trying to do chores? Must Ben, who is now covered in glory, always be a worry to me?'

'Not only you, Mother,' Elspeth said gently. 'He'll also always be a worry to me and Archibald. I need only list next year's adventures to make you realise that his company would totally ruin them . . .'

'For instance,' butted in Archibald, 'next spring, me and Elspeth plan to go down to the creek to tickle trout. Can't you imagine how many ways Ben could spoil that adventure? Then there's the summer outing. While me and Elspeth are turning over the rotting logs to see what skulks underneath, what will Ben do? Then there is our moose-calling expedition next autumn. Ben would turn it into a joke, Mother . . .'

'Not to mention our winter adventure,' interrupted Elspeth. 'Me and Archibald plan to nibble holes in the beaver dams and leave the beavers high and dry. Now,

77

Mother, can you honestly say that Ben wouldn't turn our plans upside-down?'

'Ben is already upside-down,' shrilled their angry mother. 'Can't you see him weeping tears into his ears? Although I love all my three small grizzly bears, I think that two of them should beg the forgiveness of God and Ben for saying such terrible words.'

On that wrathful note, the family settled down to sleep the winter through. Mother dreamed about doing chores without Ben under her paws. Elspeth and Archibald dreamed about their future Benless adventures. As for Ben, he stood on his head in his favourite corner of the cave, weeping tears into his ears, hoping and praying that Elspeth and Archibald would change their minds and take him adventuring when the green buds burst from the trees again. But there was really no contest. For even the gods above were betting that when the time came, Ben would not be left behind to get under his mother's paws . . .